Tiny Rabbit's
BIG WISH

Margarita Engle

Illustrated by David Walker

Houghton Mifflin Harcourt
Boston   New York

For Jake and Izabella —M.E.

Especially for Sydney and Olivia —D.W.

I thank God for wishes great and small. For the Afro-Cuban folktale that inspired this little story, I am indebted to *Mitología Cubana* by Samuel Feijoo. Love and gratitude to Curtis Engle, Victor and Kristan Engle, and Nicole and Amish Karanjit. For treasured encouragement, special thanks to Teresa Mlawer, Sylvia Vardell, Joan Schoettler, and Petunia's Place. Profound thanks to Reka Simonsen and the entire Houghton Mifflin Harcourt publishing team.

The artwork in this book was created by hand using acrylic paints on paper.
The text type was set in Joppa.

Library of Congress Cataloging-in-Publication Data is available.
ISBN 978-0-547-85286-7

Manufactured in China
SCP 10 9 8 7 6 5 4 3 2 1
4500446336

A tiny rabbit dreamed . . .

of growing as **huge**

as the forest

with legs as TALL

as trees

and eyes the size

of mOOns.

He wished for a nose as long

as an elephant's trunk . . .

and he wished for a tail as

GIGANTIC

as a mountain.

Tiny rabbit wished and wished . . .

but no matter how

ENORMOUS

his big wish grew,

he was still

tiny.

So he wished some more,
and while he was wishing,
time passed
and he grew . . .

but he grew only

a little bit.

So tiny rabbit
wished and wished
that he could grow
as SKY-HIGH
as a giraffe,

and he did grow . . .

but he grew only
to the height
of a slightly
taller
small rabbit.

So tiny rabbit
started wishing to grow
as **POWERFUL** as a gorilla . . .

but instead, he grew only

two

long,

TALL,

POWERFUL

ears

to help him hear

every loud

or quiet

SOUND

in the forest.

Tiny rabbit's big ears
helped him hear
rhinos stomping . . .

eagles screeching . . .

frogs trumpeting . . .

thunder booming . . .

branches crashing . . .

and a mischievous monkey

cheerfully chatting.

Tiny rabbit
could even hear
leaves rustling,
beetle jaws crunching,
and butterfly wings
flapping.

Best of all, tiny rabbit's
wonderful ears

could always hear

whenever a **huge**

hungry lion

was near . . .

so that tiny rabbit could

jump . . .

thump . . .

hop . . .

to his tiny,

cozy,

safe,

hidden

rabbit den . . .